Victoria Chess
ALFRED'S ALPHABET WALK

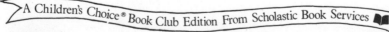
A Children's Choice® Book Club Edition From Scholastic Book Services

Greenwillow Books A Division of William Morrow & Company, Inc., New York

This book belongs to

children's choice®

To my mother and father

On Saturday morning, Alfred's mother told him to stay in the front yard and learn all the letters from A to Z.

But Alfred hid the alphabet book in
a tree trunk and ran right out of the yard.

Alfred tiptoed by two **A**ncient
Alligators so **A**s not to disturb them.

He came to a tree full of **B**rown **B**ats
hanging **B**ottoms up and heads **B**elow.

On the riverbank sat some **C**urious **C**ats **C**atching **C**rabs. They **C**alled hello to him.

Down the road was a **D**readful **D**og.
He **D**id not call hello.
He growled instead.

Alfred stopped to watch **E**ight **E**gret
Eggs as they were about to hatch.

And **F**ive **F**lying **F**ish
Flew right over his head.

He walked on and soon came
to a **G**roup of **G**ray **G**orillas.
They were all **G**rinning.

A **H**erd of **H**ungry **H**ogs
were **H**urrying **H**ome.

An **I**guana sat **I**n some **I**vy eating an **I**ce.
He **I**nvited Alfred to have one too.

Alfred said good-bye to the iguana
and soon came to a **J**uggling **J**aguar
under a **J**uniper tree.

He helped a **K**angaroo
named **K**ate to fly a **K**ite.

A **L**azy **L**ion was **L**apping water
near a **L**ily patch. Alfred crept past him.

He rested a **M**oment and asked directions
of a **M**ole who lived in a **M**ound of earth.
But the **M**ole **M**umbled so **M**uch that
Alfred could not understand him.

A **N**ightingale **N**ibbling
Nasturtiums did **N**ot **N**otice Alfred.

But some **O**dd, **O**ld **O**wls **O**n
an **O**ak branch **O**gled him.

A **P**aunchy **P**orcupine **P**icnicking alone
invited Alfred to join him. "Thank you,"
said Alfred, "but I'm not hungry."

Alfred walked on and came to a grove of **Q**uince trees. A **Q**uarrelsome **Q**ueen bee came buzzing by, so he did not pick any **Q**uinces.

Some **R**abbits were playing
Ring-around-the-**R**osy, and
he played too, for a while.

A **S**illy **S**loth **S**noozing in the **S**hade
of a **S**umac tree didn't even wake up.

A **T**ortoise and a **T**oad were **T**rying
To **T**oss **T**iddledywinks into a **T**op hat.

Alfred stopped to say hello to his
cousin **U**mberto who was sitting
Under an **U**mbrella.

And then chatted awhile with
his friend the **V**enomous **V**iper,
who offered him some **V**iolets.

Alfred met a **W**olf and a **W**olverine going for a **W**alk. He **W**ent part of the **W**ay **W**ith them.

It was getting dark and Alfred tripped over a no e**X**it sign in the **Y**ard where the **Y**ak lived.

He was frightened by a **Z**ebra and
a **Z**oril who chased him **Z**ealously,
and he decided it was time to go home.

When he got to his house, his mother asked him where he had been all day.

Alfred smiled and said,
"Out for a walk." And he recited
all the letters from A to Z. His mother
was so pleased she hugged him.

Look Who's Part of the Children's Choice® Family!

Something special for Children's Choice® Book Club members

You can get all these storybook favorites—Puss in Boots, Babar, Curious George, Lyle, George and Martha and The Year at Maple Hill Farm—to hang up on your wall. They're big (17″ × 22″) and beautiful posters, printed in full color on high quality paper. Best of all, you can get all 6 for just $3.95, including postage and handling.

To order your set of 6 Children's Choice® posters, please send your name, address and $3.95 in check or money order to:

**CHILDREN'S CHOICE® POSTERS
2931 East McCarty St.
P.O. Box 1068
Jefferson City, Mo. 65102**

Please allow 3-6 weeks for delivery. Your posters are mailed in a tube, so they won't be creased at all.

Offer expires December 31, 1981